WITHDRAWN

W9-BZX-977

Little, Brown and Company

Hachette Book Group USA
237 Park Avenue, New York, NY 10017
Visit our Web site at www.lb-kids.com

First Little, Brown and Company Edition: November 2008

First published by Doubleday Books, Inc., in 1962

Library of Congress Catalog Number: 2008921553

10 9 8 7 6 5 4 3 2 1

IM
Printed in Singapore

NIGHT'S NICE

by Barbara and Ed Emberley

LITTLE, BROWN AND COMPANY
Books for Young Readers
New York   Boston

Night's nice for making a wish,
And here's the reason why:
You can wish when you see
The first star in the sky.

Here's the Big Dipper
And moon shining bright.
You wouldn't get to see them
If there were no night.

Fireflies
Owls
And yellow-eyed cats
All think night's nice
And of course
So do bats.

Night's nice for rockets
That light up the sky
With a boom-popping racket
On the Fourth of July.

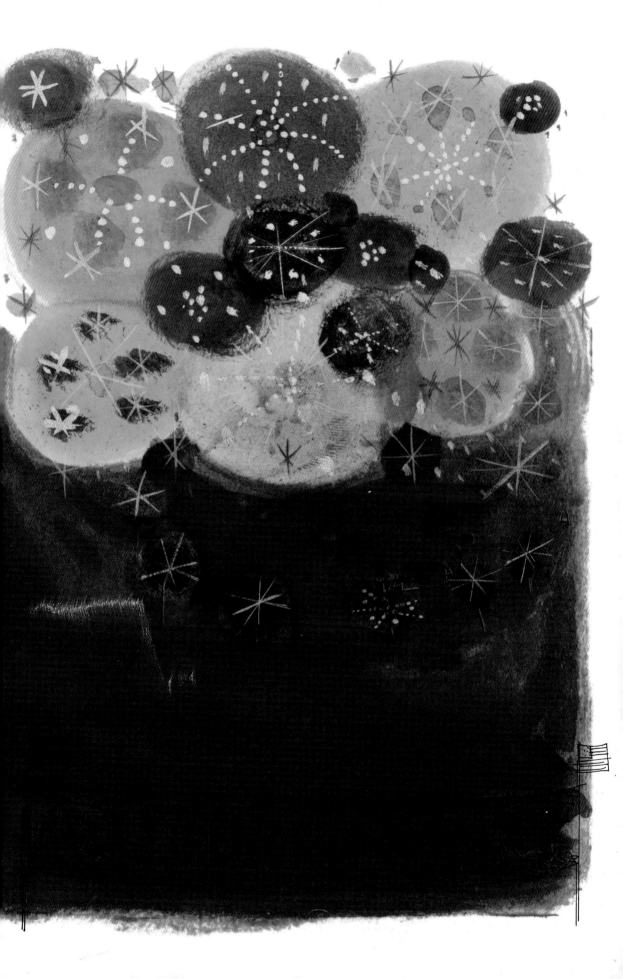

Night's nice
For spooky
Halloween make-believe,

Night's nice for carols

And snow Christmas Eve.

These lights are sea lights,
Blinking and pretty
But wait till you see
All the lights . . .

In the city.

Night's nice for sleeping,
For lions and snails
Turtles and tigers
And . . .

GIGANTIC WHALES.

For kings and for kittens,
For birds in a tree.
Night's nice for sleeping
For you and for me.

So hop into bed,
Turn over thrice
And whisper this softly:

Night's nice, night's nice, night's nice.

Good Night.